D1393249

Special thanks to
Narinder Dhami

ORCHARD BOOKS
338 Euston Road, London NW1 3BH
Orchard Books Australia
Level 17/207 Kent Street, Sydney, NSW 2000
A Paperback Original

First published in 2003 by Orchard Books.

© 2008 Rainbow Magic Limited.
A HIT Entertainment company. Rainbow Magic
is a trademark of Rainbow Magic Limited.
Reg. U.S. Pat. & Tm. Off. And other countries.
www.rainbowmagiconline.com

HiT entertainment

Illustrations © Georgie Ripper 2003

A CIP catalogue record for this book is available
from the British Library.

ISBN 978 1 84362 021 1
20

Printed in Great Britain

Orchard Books is a division of Hachette Children's Books,
an Hachette Livre UK company

www.hachettelivre.co.uk

Izzy
the Indigo
Fairy

by Daisy Meadows

illustrated by Georgie Ripper

ORCHARD

Cold winds blow and thick ice form,
I conjure up this fairy storm.
To seven corners of the mortal world
the Rainbow Fairies will be hurled!

I curse every part of Fairyland,
with a frosty wave of my icy hand.
For now and always, from this fateful day,
Fairyland will be cold and grey!

Ruby, Amber, Saffron and Fern
and Sky are safe at last.
But where is
Izzy the Indigo Fairy?

Contents

A Fairytale Beginning

"Rain, rain, go away," Rachel Walker sighed. "Come again another day!"

She and her friend Kirsty Tate stared out of the attic window. Raindrops splashed against the glass, and the sky was full of purply-black clouds.

"Isn't it a horrible day?" Kirsty said. "But it's nice and cosy in here."

She looked round Rachel's small attic
bedroom. There was just room for a
brass bed with a patchwork quilt, a
comfy armchair and an old bookshelf.

"You know what the weather on
Rainspell is like," Rachel pointed out.
"It might be hot and sunny very soon!"
Both girls had come to Rainspell
Island on holiday. The Walkers
were staying in Mermaid Cottage,
while the Tates were in Dolphin
Cottage next door.

Kirsty frowned. "Yes, but what about Izzy the Indigo Fairy?" she asked. "We have to find her today."

Rachel and Kirsty shared a wonderful secret. They were trying to find the seven Rainbow Fairies who had been cast out of Fairyland by evil Jack Frost. Fairyland would be cold and grey until all seven fairies had been found again.

Rachel thought of Ruby, Amber, Saffron, Fern and Sky, who were all safe now in the pot-at-the-end-of-the-rainbow. They only had Izzy the Indigo Fairy and Heather the Violet Fairy left to find. But how could they look for them while they were stuck indoors?

"Remember what the Fairy Queen said?" she reminded Kirsty.

Kirsty nodded. "She said the magic would come to us." Suddenly she looked scared. "Maybe the rain is Jack Frost's magic. Maybe he's trying to stop us finding Izzy."

"Oh no!" Rachel said. "Let's hope it stops soon. But what shall we do while we're waiting?"

Kirsty thought for a moment. Then she went over to the bookshelf. It was filled with dusty, old books, and she pulled one out. It was so big, she had to use two hands to hold it. "*The Big Book of Fairy Tales,*" Rachel read out, looking at the cover.

"If we can't find fairies, at least we can read about them!" Kirsty grinned.

The two girls sat down on the bed and put the book on their knees. Kirsty was about to turn the first page when Rachel gasped. "Kirsty, look at the cover! It's purple. A really deep bluey-purple."

"That's indigo," Kirsty whispered. "Oh, Rachel! Do you think Izzy could be trapped inside?"

"Let's see," Rachel said. "Hurry up, Kirsty. Open the book!"

But Kirsty had spotted something else. "Rachel," she said shakily. "It's *glowing*."

Rachel looked. Kirsty was right. Some pages in the middle of the book were gleaming with a soft bluey-purple light.

Kirsty opened the book. The ink on the pages was glowing indigo. For a moment Kirsty thought that Izzy might fly out of the pages, but there was no sign of her. On the first page was a picture of a wooden soldier. Above the picture were the words: *The Nutcracker*.

"Oh!" Rachel said. "I know this story. I went to see the ballet at Christmas."

"What's it about?" Kirsty asked.

"Well, a girl called Clara gets a wooden nutcracker soldier for Christmas," Rachel explained. "He comes to life and takes her to the Land of Sweets." They looked down at a brightly-coloured picture of a Christmas tree. A little girl was asleep beside it, holding a wooden soldier.

On the next page there was a picture of snowflakes whirling and swirling through a dark forest. "Aren't the pictures great?" Kirsty said. "The snow looks so real."

Rachel frowned. For a moment, she thought the snowflakes were moving. Gently she put out her hand and touched the page. It felt cold and wet!

"Kirsty," she whispered. "It *is* real!" She held out her hand. There were white snowflakes on her fingers.

Kirsty looked down at the book again, her eyes wide. The snowflakes started to swirl from the book's pages, right into the bedroom, slowly at first, then faster and faster. Soon the snowstorm was so thick, Rachel and Kirsty couldn't see a thing. But they could feel themselves being swept up into the air by the spinning snow cloud.

Rachel yelled to Kirsty, "Why haven't we hit the bedroom ceiling?"

Kirsty reached for Rachel's hand. "Because it's magic!" she whispered.

The Land of Sweets

Suddenly the snowflakes stopped swirling.
Rachel and Kirsty found themselves
standing in a forest, with their rucksacks
at their feet. Tall trees loomed around
them and crisp white snow covered
the ground. They certainly weren't in
Rachel's bedroom any more.

Then Rachel realised where they were.

"Kirsty, this is the forest that was in the picture," she said, grabbing her friend's arm. "We're *inside* the book!"

Kirsty looked even more scared. "Do you think Jack Frost brought us here?" she asked. "Or his goblins?" Jack Frost's goblins were always trying to stop Rachel and Kirsty from finding the Rainbow Fairies.

"I don't know," Rachel replied. Then she frowned. There was something odd about this snow. She bent down and gently touched a snowdrift. "This isn't snow," she laughed. "It's icing sugar!"

"What?" Kirsty looked amazed. She scooped up a handful and tasted it. The icing sugar was cool and sweet.

"Maybe this isn't Jack Frost's magic after all," Rachel said. "I wonder where this forest is?"

"What's that?" Kirsty asked, pointing.

Rachel could see a pink and gold glow through the trees. "Let's go and find out," she said.

They picked up their rucksacks and set
off. It was hard walking through the icing
sugar. Soon their trainers were covered in
the sugary snow.

Crack!

Rachel nearly jumped out of her skin as
a loud noise echoed through the trees.

"Sorry," said Kirsty. "I trod on a
twig."

"Wait," Rachel whispered. "I just
heard voices!"

"Goblins?" Kirsty whispered back,
looking scared again.

Rachel listened. The voices were
louder now. She sighed with relief. "No,
they sound too sweet and soft to be
goblins' voices."

Rachel and Kirsty hurried towards the
edge of the forest. When they came out
of the trees, they saw that the glow was
coming from a dazzling pink and gold
archway.

"Look, Kirsty," Rachel
gasped. "It's made
of sweets!"

Kirsty stared.
The archway
was made
of pink
marshmallows
and golden
toffees.

Then they heard the voices again. They spun round to see who it was. Two people dressed in fluffy, white coats were chatting to each other and scooping icing sugar into shiny metal buckets.
They had round, rosy cheeks and little, pointy ears. They were so busy they hadn't noticed Rachel and Kirsty yet.

"I think they're elves," Kirsty whispered. "But they're the same size as we are. That means we must be fairy- or, at least, elf-sized again."

"We haven't got any wings this time, though," Rachel whispered back.

Suddenly one of the elves
spotted them. She
looked very
surprised. "Hello!"
she called.
"Where did you
come from?"

"I'm Rachel and this
is Kirsty," Rachel explained.
"We came here through the forest."

"Where are we?" Kirsty asked.

"This is the entrance to the Land of
Sweets," said the first elf. "My name is
Wafer, and this is my sister, Cornet."

"We're the ice-cream makers," added
Cornet. "What are you doing here?"

"We're looking for Izzy the Indigo
Fairy," Kirsty told them. "Have you
seen her?"

Both elves shook their heads. "We've heard of the Rainbow Fairies," said Wafer. "But Fairyland is far away from here, across the Lemonade Ocean."

"Maybe you should ask the Sugarplum Fairy for help," Cornet suggested. "She's so clever and kind, she'll know what to do. She lives on the other side of the village."

"Could you take us to her?" Rachel asked eagerly.

The elves nodded. "Follow us," they said together. And they led Rachel and

Kirsty through the archway of pink and gold sweets.

On the other side of the arch, the sun shone down warmly from a bright blue sky. Flowers made of strawberry cream grew beneath milk-chocolate trees. Squashy pink and white marshmallow houses lined the village street, which was paved with boiled sweets.

"Isn't this great?" Kirsty laughed. "It's like being inside a giant sweet shop!"

"And it all looks *yummy!*" Rachel agreed, spotting a garden gate made of stripy rock.

There were elves hurrying everywhere. Some had shiny buckets like the ice-cream makers, and others carried tiny, silver hammers. There were gingerbread men too, looking very smart in their bright bow ties and currant buttons. Then a whole line of tiny wooden soldiers, with polished black boots, marched across the street in front of them and Rachel spotted a glistening pink sugar mouse scurrying between their feet. Kirsty and Rachel smiled at each other with delight.

The two elves led Rachel and Kirsty
down the street. Suddenly a cross-looking
gingerbread man hurried out of one of the
houses and bumped into Cornet.

"Hello, Buttons," Wafer said. "You're
in a hurry."

"What's the matter?" Cornet asked.
"You look upset."

The gingerbread man held out his
hand. "Look at my best bow tie!" he
said. "It was red when I hung it out to dry
on my washing line, and
now it's *this* colour!"

29

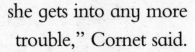

Rachel and Kirsty gasped. The bow tie
was bluey-purple!

"Izzy!" they both said together.

The ice-cream elves looked puzzled.

"I think this means that Izzy the Indigo
Fairy is close by," Rachel explained.

"We'd better help you find her before
she gets into any more
trouble," Cornet said.
Then she frowned
as a small boy elf
ran towards them.
He had one hand
clapped over his
mouth, and he was laughing.

"Scoop!" called Wafer. She turned
to Rachel and Kirsty. "He's our little
brother," she explained. "Scoop, what are
you giggling about?"

Still laughing, Scoop took his hand
away from his mouth. Rachel and Kirsty
stared. The little elf's mouth
was stained indigo!

"What's happened?" gasped Cornet.
"I had a drink from the lemonade
fountain," Scoop said between giggles.
"All the lemonade's turned bluey-purple.
It made my tongue tingle, too!"
"That sounds like more Rainbow Fairy
magic!" Kirsty said.

"Where's the lemonade fountain?"
Rachel asked the elves.

"In the village square," replied Cornet.
"Just round the corner."

"Thanks for your help," said Kirsty.
She grabbed Rachel's hand and they
ran off.

As soon as Rachel and Kirsty
rounded the corner, they skidded to
a halt. In the middle of the village
square was a pretty fountain. Bright
bluey-purple liquid bubbled up from a
fountain shaped like a dolphin. A
crowd of elves, soldiers and gingerbread
men stood round the fountain, all
talking at once. They sounded cross.
A polka-dotted Jack-in-the-Box
bounced back and forth with a grumpy
look on his face.

A swirl of indigo fairy dust shot up
from the middle of the crowd. As the
dust fell to the ground, it changed into
dewberry-scented inkdrops.

Rachel and Kirsty stared at each
other in delight. They knew what fairy
dust meant. They had found another
Rainbow Fairy!

Look Out!

"Izzy!" Rachel called, as she and Kirsty pushed their way through the crowd. "Is that you?"

"Who's that?" called a cheeky, tinkling voice.

Izzy was standing by the edge of the lemonade fountain. She had neat blue-black hair and twinkling, dark blue eyes.

She was dressed in indigo denim jeans and a matching jacket, covered with spangly patches. Inkdrop-shaped silver earrings hung in her ears, and her wand was indigo, tipped with silver.

The fairy stared at Rachel and Kirsty with her hands on her hips. "Who are you?" she asked. "And how do you know my name?"

"I'm Kirsty, and this is Rachel," Kirsty explained. "We've come to take you back to your Rainbow sisters."

"We've found five of your sisters so far," Rachel added. "We're going to help you all go home to Fairyland."

"That's brilliant news!" Izzy cried. "I've been so worried."

"How did you get to the Land of Sweets?" Kirsty asked.

"The wind blew me down the chimney of Mermaid Cottage, and into the story of *The Nutcracker*," Izzy replied. "I've been in the Land of Sweets ever since. I can't go back to Fairyland and break Jack Frost's spell without my sisters. I have to get back to Rainspell Island first."

Before Rachel and Kirsty could say
anything else, the crowd started shouting
again.

"Look what she's done to the lemonade
fountain!" grumbled one elf.

Izzy grinned at him. "I didn't
mean to," she said. "The
lemonade looked so yummy,
I just had to have a drink.
And that's when it turned indigo."

"And what about my bow tie?"
snapped Buttons. He had followed Kirsty
and Rachel to the fountain.

"I was really tired after walking out of
the forest," Izzy explained.
"I borrowed your lovely bow tie to wrap
round me while I had a little nap."

The crowd started to mutter crossly
again.

Quickly Rachel stepped forward.
"Wait," she said. "Have you heard
about the Rainbow Fairies and Jack
Frost's spell?"

The crowd listened as Rachel told
them the whole story. When she'd
finished, they didn't look cross any more.

"I'm *so* sorry for all the trouble I've
caused," Izzy said. "Please can you
tell us how to get back to Rainspell
Island?"

"The Sugarplum Fairy will help you," said the Jack-in-the-Box, with a little bounce. "Her home is just past the jellybean fields."

"That's where we were going," Kirsty said.

"Come on, then!" Izzy cried. She darted forward and took Rachel and Kirsty by the hand.

"Good luck!" called everyone.

Rachel and Kirsty walked along the
road towards the jellybean fields with
Izzy darting eagerly ahead of them. Just
outside the village was a huge
rock of golden toffee, as tall as a
marshmallow house. Elves were
tapping the rock with little hammers
to break pieces off the toffee. Other elves
picked them up and put them
into silver buckets.

Kirsty nudged Rachel. "That looks like hard work," she said. "They don't seem to be collecting much toffee at all!"

Rachel peeped into one of the buckets as an elf walked past. Kirsty was right. There were only a few chips of toffee in it.

"Is there something wrong with the toffee?" Izzy wondered.

The elf with the bucket overheard her. "It's really hard today," he grumbled. "Anyone would think it had been *frozen*."

"Frozen!" Kirsty said in alarm. "Do you think that means Jack Frost's goblins are here, in the Land of Sweets?" Whenever the goblins were close by, they brought frost and icy weather.

Izzy looked scared. "I hope not," she said.

Just then, a loud, rumbling noise and a shout of "Look out!" made them all jump. An enormous wooden barrel was rolling down the street, straight towards them! And running behind it were two goblins, grinning all over their ugly faces.

Stop Those Goblins!

"We've got you now, Izzy!" shouted one
of the goblins.

For a moment everyone froze. Then
Izzy leaped into action and gave Rachel
and Kirsty a push. "Quick! Get out of
the way!" she yelled.

They jumped aside just in time.
The elves dropped their hammers and

buckets. They dashed out of the way,
bumping into each other in their panic.

Crash!

The barrel smashed right into the toffee
mountain. Then it burst open. Lemon
sherbet spilled out in a sticky yellow
cloud.

"Izzy! Kirsty!" Rachel coughed,
peering through the sherbet. "Are

you all right?"

"I think so!" Kirsty sneezed. *"Atishoo!"*

"HELP!"

Kirsty heard Izzy's frightened voice. But she couldn't see her through the sherbet cloud.

"Help!" Izzy shouted again. "The goblins have got me!" Her voice was getting fainter.

"Quick, Rachel!" Kirsty gasped.
"Have you got our magic bags?"

Still coughing, Rachel swung her
rucksack off her back. Titania, the
Fairy Queen, had given the girls bags
full of magic gifts to help them rescue
the missing Rainbow Fairies.

Rachel opened her rucksack. Inside
it, one of the magic bags was glowing,
faintly silver. Rachel pulled out a folded
paper fan from the bag.
Puzzled, she opened the fan up.

It was coloured like the most beautiful
rainbow, with stripes
of red, orange,
yellow, green,
blue, indigo and
violet.

Rachel thought for a moment. Then she began to flap the fan at the clouds of sherbet.

Whoosh!

A blast of air from the fan blew almost all of the sherbet away.

"Wow! This fan is amazing!" Rachel gasped, as the last of the sherbet drifted off.

"Look, Rachel!" shouted Kirsty. "They're over there!"

The goblins had tied Izzy's trainers together with strawberry bootlaces. They were half-dragging, half-carrying her up the road, towards the jellybean fields.

"We've got to save her," Rachel said, quickly folding the fan and putting it in her pocket. "Come on, Kirsty!"

"I'll go and tell the Sugarplum Fairy," said one of the elves, and he dashed off.

Rachel and Kirsty ran up the road. The goblins had got a head start, but Izzy was wriggling so much that she was slowing them down.

The road led through the jellybean fields. Tall green plants stood in rows, each one covered with different-coloured beans – pink, white, blue-spotted and chocolate brown ones. Elves were picking the jellybeans and putting them into big baskets.

Suddenly, Rachel noticed that the goblins were looking greedily at the jellybeans. One of them skidded to a halt. He leaned over the fence and grabbed a big handful of beans from the nearest plant. The other goblin did the same.

"Yummy!" said the first goblin, stuffing the beans into his mouth.

"They're so greedy!" Rachel panted.

"Yes, but it gives us a chance of catching them up!" Kirsty puffed. She started to run even faster.

The elves working in the field shouted angrily at the goblins. But that didn't stop them. They gobbled down one bean after another, picking beans with one hand and holding on to Izzy with the other.

"I've got an idea," Rachel whispered to Kirsty. At the side of the road she could see some baskets full of beans which had already been picked. She hurried over and lifted up a basket. Then she held it out towards the goblins.

"Look what I've got," she called. "A whole basket full of beans!"

A Very Suitable Punishment

The goblins' eyes lit up
when they saw the basket.
Izzy grinned and winked
at Kirsty and Rachel. She'd
guessed what they were doing.

"Those jellybeans look
yummy," Izzy said to the
goblins. "I wish I could have one."

"Be quiet," snapped the goblin with the bigger nose. He turned to the other goblin. "You keep hold of the fairy while I get the beans."

"No," said the other one. "You'll eat all the beans! You hold the fairy, and *I'll* get the beans."

"No!" roared the first goblin. "Then *you'll* eat all the beans!"

Glaring at each other, both goblins let go of Izzy and ran towards Rachel.

 She quickly threw a handful of beans on the ground and backed away. The goblins bent down to grab the beans. When they stood up again, Rachel threw another handful back down the hill, away from Izzy.

Those greedy goblins just couldn't resist the yummy beans!

While the goblins were busy stuffing themselves, Kirsty rushed over to untie Izzy. "Are you all right?" she asked.

Izzy nodded and wriggled her feet. "Thank you!"

Rachel put the basket on the ground and ran over to Kirsty and Izzy. The goblins pounced on the basket and began squabbling over the rest of the beans.

"Let's get out of here!" Rachel said.
Suddenly there was a gentle flapping
noise overhead. Rachel looked up to
see a huge butterfly with pink and gold
wings fluttering above them. On its back
sat a fairy with long, red hair.

The butterfly landed gently on the ground. The fairy climbed off the butterfly's back and smiled at Izzy and the girls. She wore a long green and gold dress and a tiara.

"Welcome," she said. "I am the Sugarplum Fairy." She looked sternly at the goblins who were crouching beside the empty bean basket. "What are *you* doing in the Land of Sweets?" she demanded.

The goblins didn't answer. They were too busy groaning and holding their tummies.

"Oooh!" moaned the one with the big nose. "My tummy hurts."

"Mine too," whined the other one. "I feel sick."

"They've eaten too many jellybeans!" Izzy grinned at Rachel and Kirsty.

The Sugarplum Fairy looked even crosser. "As you have stolen so many of our delicious jellybeans," she said to the goblins, "you must be taught a lesson."

"Why don't you make them pick jellybeans?" Izzy suggested.

"What a good idea," smiled the Sugarplum Fairy.

"That doesn't seem like a very bad punishment," Kirsty whispered to Rachel.

"But just look at the goblins' faces," Rachel whispered back.

The goblins looked horrified at the
thought of more jellybeans! They tried to
get up, as if they wanted to run away.
But the Sugarplum Fairy waved her
hand and several elves came running out
of the jellybean fields. They marched the
goblins into the nearest field and handed
them empty baskets. With sulky faces,
the goblins started to pick the beans.

"Serves them right!" laughed Izzy. Then she looked worried again. "But I still need to get back to my Rainbow sisters."

"Please can you help us get back to Rainspell Island?" Rachel asked the Sugarplum Fairy.

The beautiful fairy nodded. "We will send you home by balloon!" she said. She waved her wand at the empty bean basket. Rachel and Kirsty watched in amazement as it grew bigger and bigger. "There is your basket."

"But where's the balloon?" said Rachel.

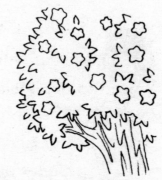

The Sugarplum
Fairy pointed to
a tall tree, covered
with pink blossoms.

"What pretty
flowers," Kirsty said.
Then she took a closer look, and began
to laugh. "They're not flowers. They're
pieces of bubblegum!"

"How is that going to help?" Rachel
felt puzzled.

Izzy grinned at them, her eyes
sparkling mischievously.
"Leave it to me!" she said.
She pulled one of the
bubblegum flowers off
the tree, popped it
into her mouth and
began to chew.

Then, screwing up her
face, she blew a huge,
pink bubblegum bubble.
She puffed and puffed,
and the bubble grew
bigger and
bigger. Soon it
towered above them.
It was the biggest
bubblegum bubble
Rachel and Kirsty
had ever seen!

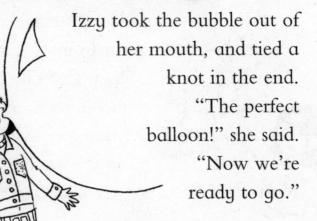

Izzy took the bubble out of
her mouth, and tied a
knot in the end.
"The perfect
balloon!" she said.
"Now we're
ready to go."

Rachel and Kirsty grinned at each other. What a brilliant way to travel back to Rainspell!

The elves working in the jellybean fields, and the elves who had followed Rachel and Kirsty out of the village, helped to tie the bubblegum balloon to the basket. Then Rachel, Kirsty and Izzy climbed inside.

65

The Sugarplum Fairy waved her wand at the balloon, showering it with gold sparkles.

"The balloon will take you to Rainspell Island," she explained. "Goodbye, and good luck."

"Thank you," called Rachel and Izzy.

But Kirsty was looking round in dismay. "There's no wind!" she said. "We won't be able to get off the ground!"

The Bubblegum Balloon

Rachel looked at the leaves on the bubblegum tree. Kirsty was right. They weren't moving at all.

The Sugarplum Fairy smiled. "Rachel, don't you remember what you have in your pocket?" she said.

"Of course!" Rachel exclaimed. "The magic fan!" She took it out of her pocket and unfolded it. Then she flapped it under the balloon.

Whoosh!

The blast of air lifted the balloon up into the sky. "Goodbye!" Kirsty called, waving at the Sugarplum Fairy and all the elves. "Thank you for all your help," Izzy called. "Sorry I made such a mess!" she added with a giggle. The balloon bobbed slowly upwards. As it got higher, the wind became stronger, so Rachel put away the fan. Big, puffy clouds began swirling around the balloon.

"We'll be home soon," Rachel said,
trying to sound cheerful.

The wind roared around them,
rocking the basket from side to side.
Rachel, Kirsty and Izzy hung on to
each other.

Then, all of a sudden, the wind
dropped. The balloon stopped swaying.
The air felt warm.

Kirsty opened her eyes. "We're home!"
she gasped.

They were back in Rachel's attic
bedroom at Mermaid Cottage. The
balloon and the basket had vanished. The
book of fairy tales was lying on the floor,
open at *The Nutcracker*.

"But where's Izzy?" Rachel said.

"I'm in here!" said a cheeky voice.
The Indigo Fairy popped up from
Rachel's pocket. She
wriggled out and
fluttered into the air,
her wings sparkling
with rainbows
and showering the
room with fairy
dust inkdrops. The
smell of dewberries
drifted up as they
popped.

Kirsty picked up the book. She turned
the pages until she found a picture of the
Land of Sweets. "It's a shame we didn't
get to taste any of those lovely sweets,"
she said.

As she spoke, a tiny puff of icing sugar floated out of the book. Then a shower of different-coloured jellybeans fell on to Rachel's bed.

"They must be a present from the Sugarplum Fairy!" laughed Izzy.

Rachel and Kirsty each popped a jellybean into their mouths. They were tiny, but they tasted lovely!

"Yum!" said Izzy, munching a bean. "Can we take some back to the pot for my sisters?"

Rachel nodded. "Let's go right away," she said, filling her pockets with beans. "Your sisters will be waiting for you." She looked at Kirsty and smiled. They had rescued another fairy and escaped the goblins once again. They'd even been inside a fairy story in a book. And now there was only one more fairy to find!

Now it's time for Rachel and Kirsty to help...

Heather the Violet Fairy

Read on for a sneak peek...

"I can't believe this is the last day of our holiday!" said Rachel Walker. She gazed up at her kite as it rose in the clear blue sky.

Kirsty Tate watched the purple kite soar above the field beside Mermaid Cottage. "But we still have to find Heather!" she reminded Rachel.

Jack Frost's wicked spell had banished the seven Rainbow Fairies to Rainspell Island. And without the Rainbow Fairies, Fairyland had no colour! Kirsty and Rachel had already found Ruby,

Amber, Saffron, Fern, Sky, and Izzy.
Now there was just Heather the Violet
Fairy left to find.

Rachel felt the kite tug on its string.
She looked up. Something violet and
silver flashed at the end of the kite's long
tail. "Look up there!" she shouted.

Kirsty shaded her eyes with her hand.
"What is it? Do you think it's a fairy?"
she asked...

Read Heather the Violet Fairy to find out
what adventures are in store for Kirsty and Rachel!

Meet the fairies, play games
and get sneak peeks at
the latest books!

There's fairy fun for everyone at

www.rainbowmagicbooks.co.uk

You'll find great activities, competitions, stories and
fairy profiles, and also a special newsletter.

Win Rainbow Magic Goodies!

There are lots of Rainbow Magic fairies, and we want to know
which one is your favourite! Send us a picture of her and tell
us in thirty words why she is your favourite and why you like
Rainbow Magic books. Each month we will put the entries into
a draw and select one winner to receive a Rainbow Magic
Sparkly T-shirt and Goody Bag!

Send your entry on a postcard to Rainbow Magic Competition,
Orchard Books, 338 Euston Road, London NW1 3BH.
Australian readers should email: childrens.books@hachette.com.au
New Zealand readers should write to Rainbow Magic Competition,
PO Box 3255, Shortland St, Auckland 1140, NZ.
Don't forget to include your name and address.
Only one entry per child.

Good luck!

Tilly the Teacher Fairy

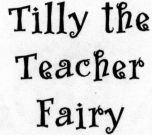

Meet Tilly the Teacher Fairy! Can Rachel and Kirsty help get her magical items back from Jack Frost and make school fun for everyone again?

www.rainbowmagicbooks.co.uk